Hell's Press Presents

ISBN   978-1-7381321-0-2   (paperback)
ISBN   978-1-7381321-9-5   (ebook)

hellspress.com

Fairie Tales

Jack and the Beanstalk

COUNT FATHOM

Dedicated to...

... you, the tired, the poor, the huddled masses yearning to breathe free, the reader with a sweet tooth, or an odd proclivity. We yearn for entertainment, and I'm here for you to serve. A tale to pass away an hour, if you like a moral curve. What some see as bent is straight, if you have eyes like mine. I see a house that tilts a bit, and I think that it's just fine.

Our Fairie Tales are watered down, as at our pearls we clutch. All our pigments turn to brown, lest we offend too much. I've come with colours from the sun to wash our stagnant skies, and clear up all the misconceptions, fibs and outright lies. See us for the first time now, as we really are. We're wicked, good and in between, some are quite bizarre. Even I, a moral grey, do think they've gone too far.

Inspired by Emma Lazarus

Table of Contents

Preface

Fie! This is the first. It's not the worst
and nor is it the best. You enter now upon
a path that proves a moral test. Jack is
something of a host, he'll take you to your
seat. He'll read by heart a wine list, and
he'll advertise the meat. A joke, a pun, a
shoulder touch, a hypnotizing guile. Beneath a spell he'll put you, unbeknownst to
you the while. Once you're set and com-
fortable, you'll think you've found your
place. But others form a queue behind to
smack you in the face.

These are tales you've heard before,
but not the way you thought. The cook is
quite creative adding spices to the pot. Hot,
you say, or bitter. Some say sweet, or tough
to chew. Pleasure comes in many forms,
is it just right for you? Promises I will not
make, for I am me, not you. I'm in the
kitchen cooking, curating your meal. You'll
feast, and when it's done you'll know you
don't know how to feel. Full you'll be, with
images, with thoughts and shock and fun.
The food in this establishment would wet
a pious nun. So settle back, relax a bit, and
taste a hot cross bun.

Jack and the Beanstalk

Through vale and valley, glen and gorge, fen and meadow and plain, as scattered as they may be varied, are all the crawling, walking, wading, warbling creatures of creation going about their doings indifferent to one another. And among all this criss-crossing life, at odds and evens, are the intersections of interaction, the interlocutions, the touching of one to another to commune, to resolve, or to entertain. How glorious the possibilities!

I will serve before you a particularly tasty treat. In this case you might think him a kind of logger. But you would be wrong. You see him there, snap snap, up a tree, right near the top. That's what loggers do, isn't it? But where's his saw? He hasn't one. He has a gob of a bag, but it's near empty. He's gathering something there. Are they nests? Why yes they are! That's the nest of a curlew. Lucky for you my ornithological competence, for the curlew is a rare bird and becoming rarer by the day. Maybe that's why Jack's bag is near empty.

The setting sun spreads marmalade across the sky, and lickety snap, what a funny chap, Jack skates down the tree like a bow legged puppet, boot spikes tap dancing down the bark to the conductor of fate, a mysterious maestro manipulating those who will submit. It's some time before our new friend reaches the threshold of his home, a small flip of farm land with a host of buried ancestry interred. A bond and a trust with their plot, nourished with generations of blood. Each corpse was a sacrifice to the kami, the jinn, the leprechaun of the land. Jack and his mother will soon join them.

Jack's mother took a long look in the bag Jack plopped on the kitchen table. Then she stuck her whole head inside. Jack heard her sobbing in there. "No, mother! I feel it! The tide of fortune is turning in our favour. The curlew told me so. Tomorrow will be better. We'll have enough nests for some salt. Then you'll see. We'll have the family affairs right soon enough."

With the bag still over her head, mother stood stalk straight facing Jack, silent for a moment. An order barked sharply at Jack, with the authority of an menacing index finger to back it up, "Go early to market with the cow. Sell her for what you can get. Bring food and the rest of the money home to me."

Up Jack got, beating the birds to breakfast, the following morn and fetched a lead for Rowina. Jack had drunk rivers of milk from the old girl since he was just a wee lad. But mother did the milking, and Rowina would nip at Jack had she the chance. Jack swore to mother about the cow, accusing the fiendish beast of cursing him with the evil eye, even going so far as to claim the steady decline of the family affairs dates back to her purchase. In fact, the cow had, indeed, been jealous of the coddling Jack received as a child, and harboured a long standing grudge against him. She was a shrewd conniver, that one, and Jack kept a distance until the impulse to torment the old lady became too strong.

Giving her a good hard slap on her bony ass, Jack and Rowina marched off down the forest path suffering some emotional confusion. Several years hence, with her eyesight failing and her hair falling out in the twilight of her life, Rowina would still find joy in reminiscence, her periodic spontaneous malevolence towards this boy who grew into a man before her very eyes. A disgrace of a man, in her opinion, always in his dreams, never his mind on where he is and what he is doing. She spit and they walked on.

Jack had not a thought in his head. But then one hit him. And he hopped up straddling Rowina backwards, erupting in gay laughter at her expense. The old girl lurched her ass against an oak, an overhanging limb knocked Jack's noggin, and Jack tumbled to the ground in a daze. A fog befell him, when just then a little old waddler bent over, brushing a bushy grey beard chin to forehead across Jack's face.

Jack was bleary. He propped himself between oak and elbow, and tried to follow the gesticulating dance and strange foreign accents of the lively little fellow before him. In a dazzling pirouette, the green dwarf flourished forth in a low bow, palm extend-

ed entreating Jack to examine. Three beans
were therein.

Submitting to the beckon of fathom-
less fate, Jack's hand received the proffered
beans. Jack fell back once more in a daze,
clutching at his banged brains in pitiful
pain, whimpering himself into a slumber
in due time. Under a spell of darkness the
mind is unshackled from beastly activity.
Into the immense unknown, carried in cur-
rents through channels and canals and over
stormy black seas sails a slumbering something, unencumbered and free. But the body
butts in and the spell is undone and we wake
enslaved once again. Up Jack got to a sunset,
puzzled at the loss of the day.

Jack is elated! He is the saviour of his
family's fortune, for clever Jack had out-

witted them all and converted that sick old cow into three magical beans. Think of the tearful penitence of his mother, he, Jack, all powerful before her. Her at this feet, on her knees in obeisance and gratitude to the shrewd unfathomed intellect of her great son, Jack!

Jack skipped across water to the very door of his home, bursting with inner pride and joy. For love of God, he wished he'd had a trumpeter, or a flugelist, or a cockerel to announce his grand arrival. "Mum! I've settled the family affairs for all time. Bow before me you filthy swine!", and his hand thrust magnificently towards the heavens, heralding the magic beans.

"You've sold the cow for a handful of beans! You rascal, child! I'll beat the life out of you for this!" swore his mother, in disgust and outrage. A slight woman, and starved gaunt by years of privation, Jack's mother yet wielded a determined, ferocious temper when her wrath was summoned. Switch in hand, the spritely red faced witch chased Jack out the room and about the yard, whipping him mercilessly, and, in his efforts to protect himself from the onslaught, Jack flailed the precious beans he knew not where.

Exhausted, panting, sweat pooling at her chin, and soaking the collar of her shirt, mother took to a chair to recover, threatening, "you just wait until your father comes home!", and Jack sighed with relief. They had heard nothing about his father for two years, since he had been conscripted to soldier in the king's army, against an obscure enemy in far flung lands. Mother was now in tears. Both retired to their rooms without a word, and starving, as they had nothing to eat.

Jack felt hard done by, and clenched his fists in resentment and wounded honour for some time before drifting off into the land of the elves. An uneasy sleep, haunted by the goblins and ghouls of the other world and their horrendous yips and moans, before coming to at what should have been the break of dawn.

But on this magical morning, looking east, the sun was nowhere to be seen. The entirety of the fiery eye was eclipsed by three enormous braided green stalks, stretching from the nourishing black earth right into the ephemeral heavens, beyond the sight of man. Jack staggered outside, arched his head back scouring the skies for an end to the magnificent growth, bopped his head against his ass and tumbled over into the dirt. An inquisitive piglet ambled by and sniffed en-thusiastically at the prone Jack, tickling the young man with its eager pumping snout.

Jack, being nimble, hopped to his feet, bent his head back once again, but knew better this time when to rein it in and didn't tumble over. Far enough that his mouth caverned open, his sight line parallel to gravity, and, yes, it happened again. His head hit his ass and he tumbled over onto the dirt, Betsy nosing pig slobber over him, moisturizer for young Jack's face. Jack hopped up.

Jack felt an inner fire ignite. Tinder to kindling to log to coal in just moments, a determination Jack had never felt the likes of before. Jack looked up a third time, and was able to remain for some time staring into the heavenly realm. He felt a wave of accomplishment ripple through, his hair an electric tingle, and his flesh bubbled like an untended pot. He wouldn't tumble over. His beans were magic. And he was the saviour of the family affairs. Jack thrust a fist skyward.

Quite sure, confident, in fact, doubts dismissed as ridiculous, Jack immediately prepared to climb to the top of this marvellous monstrosity. The fruits of his finest financial philosophy finalized to fantastic satisfaction. This stalk was fortune's hand reaching down to him, fate bending to offer

him all his merry heart may desire, were he
only to take that chance.

Without waiting to wake mother,
Jack pranced into action, snatching the
gob of a bag with three final curlew nests,
some string and a knife to help manage the
transportation of all his hopes and dreams.
Strapping on and lacing up his climbing
boots, Jack attacked his task with all the
enthusiasm of the unrelenting optimist. He
was a good tall tree up in a snap, and two in
two more. Snap snap. He kept that pace up
for a snap and eight more, but from thence
he slowed markedly, taking four snaps, then
ten for a tree of fair height.

What a marvel!, thought Jack, as
he climbed the bare root. For it started to
sprout, first sparsely, then densely, the most

varied and glorious of mother earth's fruit. Up up, up the day passed, stopping once for a bite. Then he hung his bag gently as a bed for the night. On and on went our Jack, his provisions ran low, but the fruit on the root were beginning to grow, to fabulous sizes until, near the end, the fruit that he found shamed a hippo's rear end.

The first three nights in the bag were the worst. A flock of sparrow or finch would often flutter by, ever curious as to Jack's intentions. They would spit and gossip the most ludicrous nonsense about fairy kingdoms and sugar candy mountains and cavernous mining dwarves and the fires of dragons and haunts of despicable evil. On days four and five visits by flock were no longer common, Jack might spend a meal

chatting with a condor or a vulture. The one
had much to say about the state of affairs,
but wouldn't go far in politics, as he lacked
all conviction in his proposed remedies,
asign of intelligence if you ask me.

Jack suspected the other was waiting
for him to fall. The vulture might peck at
Jack's socks, claiming to unburden him of a
briar, or it might bump Jack as he climbed,
pardon having forgotten his spectacles. The
vulture, however, was a rhetorician of tre-
mendous and frightening ability.

"I am despised, for I feed on the flesh
of the dead. My handsome, splendid features
are unappreciated. I glisten with secretion,
adapted for my most perfect survival, and
I am accused of being unclean. The herd of

bleating sheep you consider enlightened is led by nothing more than appetite."

Here the vulture, gaped wide his beak and snapped shut again, a shade from Jack's cheek.

"You scramble over one another, worse than rats escaping a fire. Towards what end? So you can sit atop the mountain of struggling flesh. Together you could accomplish so much, were you in tune. How can you be, when you have undermined nature's greatest gift – the survival of the fittest. The weak have been dragged forward generation by generation through the greed of your state, as workers create wealth. Those that would naturally die off now pollute your stream beyond hope."

The tightly squinting vulture hack hacked out a phlegmatic squirt of sticky spit, and dropped it onto the world below.

"You reward greed, self-interest, deception, and insincerity. Your species is a disease, You have poisoned our world, and I am disgusted with you. I wait for your death, Jack, with great anticipation. I will enjoy tearing your guts from your body and spreading them wide for my amusement. Your suffering and humiliation will atone for the sins of your kind."

When he had climbed high enough to leave the vulture below, Jack was im-mensely relieved.

After a week of nights in the bag, only the rarest and noblest of animals, true philosophers, were to be met. A majestic crane spent much of the second week visiting Jack regularly, between feedings. They were above the highest peak at this point, and the air was stranglingly thin. The winds at the higher altitudes were terrifying. Luckily, Jack had neglected to cut his nails for some time past, and was able to latch himself to the now thinning beanstalk securely. At such times as the winds forced Jack into one spot, the crane, a benevolent creature and sociable as well, would encircle Jack in a wing cocoon, where they would whisper to one another, sometimes for hours, until the fates allowed Jack to continue his climb.

"What you see before you is a mirage," the crane had said, "you are incapable of perceiving the true nature of matter, and the subtle tangle of woven forces that comprise the fabric of our reality. You live in a world of shadow. Within a very narrow beam of visible light, you say you see all. You are wrong. All your technological wizardry, while clever, is hopelessly limited and will end in a paradox of multiplicity. The forces of the higher dimensions are immeasurable from your relative position."

Jack felt not lost in the presence of the crane, despite the inevitability of his ignorance revealed. "But don't lose heart! All of us have enough. We can feel the harmonic pulse of life propagating through land, air, and sea, and, in fact, space and time. You must blend your life sound into the great symphony of all. And you, Jack, have done so."

"Destiny guides the heart. Every time you have submitted to her call, you have thrust a fist triumphantly into the air. You are following strings of fate, as you should, through a web far too grand in scale for your comprehension. When we resist, we deviate, we encounter obstruction and difficulty. Your stubborn free will is an debilitating impediment to your natural progress. I shed tears for the tragic fate of humanity. Such gifts squandered on shit throwing apes."

Here the crane left off for some time, staring into the unobscured nothingness, swaddled in the howling of eternity.

"Am I to gain my treasure? My reward for my acquiescence? Will I be rich as a king?"

"Yes, Jack. Your reward awaits you in the heavenly spheres. I will leave you now. Follow, don't lead."

And with that the crane flew off into the mist. The mist? Jack was enveloped in a suffocating greyness. He was overcome, momentarily, by a shiver of terror, and clutched desperately to the stalk, eyes clenched, whispering for mother and mercy.

Some minutes passed, and Jack felt a little silly, his fingers dug in two knuckles deep, choking the plant with his thighs, and the sweat of fear pouring out of him. The great beanstalk carried on upward for only four snaps more, before dwindling to a fine tip. Unclenching his eyes to a surprise, Jack was but the width of a man from solid ground. Where did that come from? Jack was puzzled. The mist had dissipated. Far beneath his feet, clouds frolicked in a merry dance, moving from partner to partner in blended motifs of dissonance and harmony. A sun bathed field lay before Jack, rolling some ways before breaking upon the bul-warks of a magnificent castle.

Jack hopped off the stalk into a forest of grass, each blade his height. This was the land of giants. How was it that from the crane to the vulture, to all their silly little cousins, all the creatures he had met had spoken knowingly of this wondrous land? Jack, of course, had heard stories about ogres and trolls, and had conversed at length with animals since his youngest memories. But this land of giants, cloaked in cloud among the heavens was beyond his imagination.

Letting his heart lead the way, Jack began with a few uncertain steps through the grass forest. Each step brought confidence, and soon Jack and his heart were racing, the blades around him bending away from the compression of the air in front of a hard -charging Jack. In this land of the gods, Jack himself had changed. He felt strong. He felt fast. He felt he was still himself, but the reliable laws of nature had altered mysteriously. He felt torrents coursing through him. Jack was immersed in an ocean of chaotic energy, which would channel through him as a river through a narrow canyon. Rapids of energy roared through Jack. Bug eyed wild, Jack zigged, zipped, and zoomed in a violent and erratic pattern known only to his soul.

And he did not go unnoticed. He was a riotous disturbance for countless residents. A ladybug, big as Jack's head, was frightened out of her wits, spun dizzy, knocked against a stick, and fell belly up in the mud. A caterpillar, munching comfortably mid way up and through a tasty blade, when Jack came storming along, breaking the blade with the force of his outstretched arm. The caterpillar fell in the most undignified and humiliating fashion, causing an outbreak of hilarity amongst the fleas and crickets and mites and hoppers nearby. And far above, within the top turret of this giant's castle, a not so fair lady spied young Jack's performance, and approved.

From deep in the bowels of the cursed dungeons came a growling big bass howl.

"Fee! Fi! Fo! Fum! I smell the blood of an Englishman. Be he alive or be he dead, I'll grind his bones to make my bread."

"Henry, you keep your filthy remarks to yourself for the rest of today. How often must I suffer these ranting outbursts of yours? This morning he was French. And they come up so irregularly, that I'll not tolerate having you stir up a hornets's nest in the castle every time your intuition whispers in your ear. If we have a visitor, you'll catch up with him soon enough. They'll be coming into the castle, after all. Express your enjoyment in silence, my dear."

She was a booming tenor. Sweet in the higher register, melodious in the low. Her sound reverberated round and down the medieval stone, and the towers sung like pipe organs in answer to the mistress. Henry, that ape, slow as he spoke, had adopted a poor posture from a young age. It was never corrected, and led to permanent muscular dystrophy, an hunched burly brutish giant, with horror and doom in his voice.

Meanwhile, Jack zoomed past the manicured garden beds, raised and inset at just Jack's height, past the spitting fountain, choreographed to some of classical music's finest, across an immense drawbridge, of wood thick as thrice the length of a man, through a closed, but porous grated iron gate, and straight up to Henry's humongous castle doors. Jack was quite small enough to squeeze under, like a blade of grass himself, and was soon zooming to his heart's desire in and out, around and under, through and between for all the treasures to be found therein. And he found his way, at last, to the top of the tallest staircase in the tallest turret of the tallest tower. And he met Magogola.

Of frightening size, one step could crush a man, Jack fixated on her enormous feet.

"Hello, my dear. I see you there." The slow melody milked out of the giant. Jack was entranced. "And where might you be from?"

Jack was stunned, but the rivers still surged through him, propelling, enforcing action. "I'm Jack! I climbed the magic beanstalk. I followed my heart to my treasure, and it has brought me to you!"

Jack scrambled up a calf, under a loose frock blindly weaseled through an elastic waistband, up and hugged her heart tight. The proustian spell fell like confetti after a pulse or two and Jack scampered down in a snap and three more. "You fine little fellow! I will give you all your heart desires. Come back to Magogola!"

Jack, again submitting to the now unstoppable force of fate, dashed straight for her toes. She shrieked as he spun and twirled and fished under and over those pot bellied pigsies. She howled and moaned in delight, and shook with an explosion of ecstasy, as Jack settled down, snuggling into a hammock between Lucy and Consuela, as he called them, pigs two and three. Magogola was thrilled with her new friend. She kept him as a pet.

Henry was grouchy about the situation. He would eat this man one day, that was understood, and reaffirmed by his other half, his sister, and his wife. Their giant life cycle is peculiar, in that an egg is fertilized once in a lifetime through perfect affection, and bears two offspring of differing sex, bound to renew their kind. The older generation die off as the younger mature. Henry and Magogola were destined to bear an egg of this kind. He, being such a brute, failed to excite her emotions, and both feared much time might pass before they could fulfill their duty. Jack was tolerated, as he clearly entertained his sister, and lifted her spirits. And he had generously endowed three curlew nests upon his hosts, considered a delicacy among the giants. But along with Henry's appetite, his jealousy would grow.

Jack rode Magogola everywhere. All over the house, and on the furniture, in practically every room, out in the garden, further afield in the trees, along magical paths, sharing with one another the splendours of life. A friendship quickly developed into a heartfelt bond, a touching of souls, and having once shared of the same waters, will forever be part of one another. Magogola felt her heart's desires fulfilled.

In return, she would lavish Jack in comfort and ease. Lobster so large that it could threaten an armada would be served meat extracted and set using the tail for a bowl, a bowl the size of a small lake for

Jack. Then for supper, steak from a beast
that could devour a rainforest would sit
like stacked mattresses on the table, as Jack
scurried around taking tiny nibbles hardly
noticeable. One impulsive day, while Jack
and Goggy, as he now referred to her, lay
in the grass by a river, his mistress removed
from her purse a lovely golden harp, but of a
size suitable to Jacl's world below. The harp
began to play a light lovely lilting little li-
bretto accompaniment all by itself. Jack was
agog. Zoom! Jack was off on a tear through
the blades once again, in joyous celebration,
fist thrust skyward.

Goggy was in tears of laughter, and
gave the harp outright to Jack as a memen-
to of her affection. Jack spun dizzy till he
dropped, and had to be carried home in the

bag with the harp, which was placed in Jack's private space, in a corner of Goggy's room. This was rather rash, as the harp, among countless other items, had been inherited by each generation of their kind over millennia. And the origins of the harp are a mystery, but I dare think Orpheus. Now it was little Jack's. Henry would not approve.

Over time Goggy came to truly love our little Jack. One purple crimson painted evening, the curtains were drawn close around our soul mates. Assumption, conjecture, and slander will tell of what was shared between them that night. But we know that Jack emerged with a very special creature as reward. Goggy gave Jack her goose, again an inheritance long ago from below. This goose shat gold eggs, one a day, a magical, fabled creature, and the undoing of empires, now sat next to the harp in Jack's corner.

Several weeks hence, Goggy began to show signs that she was with egg. And Henry caught on.

"Fee! Fie! Fo! Fum! Englishman for crust and crumb. When I find Jack, he's good and dead! I'll grind his bones to make my bread. And wash him down with fog and rum!"

Bullish Henry bounced off walls while cornering at alarming speed, over and over again, the very castle itself began to tremble. And he didn't stop, charging from room to room, thundering bloody murder as he went. Creatures for leagues around took shelter at the frightful eruption. Irate and irrational, Henry went to blazes and back, while Magogola had time to secure an escape for her beloved.

Jack was terrified. Goggy rushed in, glistening and breathless. A wordless panic gripped them. Then Jack held up his string. He tied it around his body, and the other end to his gob of a bag, now carriage for the harp and the well mannered goose. Jack hopped into his toe hammock. The fear ebbed, and confidence took hold. They were off.

Only steps from the door to the castle, and crashing in ferocious and wild comes unhinged Henry. He seizes Magogola at the elbows in a vice and lifts her clear from the stones.

"I'll have that English rat tonight!" roars Henry, frantic. Then with a broken miserable melancholy howl, "Where is he?"

Henry dropped Goggy plop on the stones, and off he went in a sobbing rage.

Goggy took a breath to steady her wounded heart, and moved off intent, through the humongous castle doors, beneath the raised grated iron gate, over the immense drawbridge, past the spitting fountain, and beyond the manicured garden beds. Goggy stood at the very precipice of her world, and the tears began to fall.

Jack would be saved, but lost forever. But forever was not so very long for her, as she knew. She had to fend for herself from such a young age that she could not remember her parents beyond their horrifying lifeless bodies, pushed out into the river. The same would happen to her. So she let her little Jack descend upon the magic vine, connecting the upper and lower worlds, with confused and crippling emotions.

Jack made haste, but was inconvenienced by the cumbersome weight of his wares. Seventy thousand seven hundred and seventy seven snaps later, from the heavens far above, in the bluest of all blue days came the vile, thundering quake, "Fee! Fie! Fo! Fum!"

Submitting to the summons of fate disguised in instinct, Jack pulls the knife from its sheath, and hacks away in a mad fever of panicked attack. Within minutes this still immature part of the vine succumbed to Jack's insanity, and a river of twisting green stalk rushed past. A booming vowel blew on the wind from above, sharper, louder, a crescendo, then Doppler shifting smoothly through the low registers, and ending in a deep reverberating pulse that shivered through Jack tip to toe. So fast as to be nearly unseen, Henry fell to his death far below in the world of men, hidden in the deepest forest, soon grown over in a thick carpet of moss and lichen, and never yet recovered.

Jack held close to the stalk, wearied and weak. Weaker by the snap. Above, the richness and wonders of the heavens dizzied Jack's mind further, and he resolved to let the matter lie until he could deliberate at lei-sure upon such glory. Jack couldn't help but look one last long moment more into the infinite possible, thrust his fist triumphantly towards the gods, when who should fly by, out of the fine blue, but his friend the crane, tipping his wings in greeting and congratulations, giving Jack a loop and diminishing into the horizon, where all things meet.

Descending ever faster, Jack fevered with excitement, his pride swelling dangerously, let his imagination run amok within his mind. "Mother! I am the saviour of the family affairs! Bow beneath me, you wretched swine!" Like a dart from a dark cloud, a blurred bullet of a bird burst by, snipping violently at the string securing Jack's plunder. Stunned, Jack in a second saw fall, and forever lost, the favours of fortune, as they had come. Miraculously. A hacking vulture guffaw rippled into time, behind a final song

from our goose, svelte and sleek, that be-
lieved she was a swan.

Jack gazed down now upon the
world, the vales and dales, the field and
furrow, the fog and frost and sadness and
death, marbled mountains a licentious
tease, a peek up mother earth's skirt , the
glassy glacial melt water forging valley into
the hardest rock, pastures and paddies and
ponies and princes and paupers alike, and
the fickle fingers of fate, whether an agent of
conscious intent or a finite riddle one might
calculate, grieve Jack must and grieve Jack
did, as down the stalk and into history he
finally and forever slid.

The End

Acknowledgments

Charles Perrault was French, it's true. Don't let that put you off. "What?" you say with scorn and sneer, a gesticulating scoff, "A French-man in acknowledgment? To him your hat you doff?"

Yes, I do, he's quite a man, for Charles I beg a truce. For in the world of Fairie Tales, Charles, you'll find, is Zeus. He was the first, among the best, at taming Mother Goose.

To Anderson I give a nod, a writer best, bar none. Fairie Tales of finest silk this author for us spun. To this man I bend the knee, I owe this man a tonne.

He fell from bed one winter day, and left us with the loss. His blood has inked these pages, and for me he is the boss. If Hans were here to read this book I'd hope he'd not be cross.

The Brother's Grimm are next in line, I'll trumpet out my praise. I owe them, too, they've set the stage, they've never left my gaze. A tribute I will pay to them, they've helped in endless ways.

The Fairie Tales are fluid and they need not be so cute. A moral incubation will deny us their true loot. The Brothers set us on the path of most delicious fruit.

Acknowledgment I pay to these and others of their kind, contributions gifted to a warped and twisted mind. The lens through which I've seen them will, I fear, be much maligned.

Author

Born into a world of sin, a hateful paradigm, I am a man that turned his back upon his place and time. Escape with me in Fairie Tales, or charge me with a crime. But read you will, cause read you must, for reading is sublime. Up through the branches of the tree the faithful souls will climb. Listen well within the tree, enlightened bells do chime. I hear them clearly in my heart, and often they do rhyme.

A journey together, in play not in haste. For hurry we mustn't, for hurry's a waste. The breath and the syllable each have a taste. If you move on too quickly, the meaning's misplaced. Like eating gourmet, but it all tastes like paste.

Savour the words in each story I tell.
The book is an organism, each word is a cell.
You need the right tools if you want to read
well. Patience is one, and irreverence is swell.
The page holds ideas, not unlike a shell, maybe
a meaning or maybe a smell, maybe encourage-
ment for you to rebel. You'll have to look twice
before bidding farewell.

One day, I am sure, I will sit on your
shelf, all knowing, all seeing, an unruly elf.
Perched in my place I will know your true self.
And you will know mine.

Hell's Press

Hell is a prison. Incarcerated within we find the embodiment of Evil. She is known by many names, here she will be Nuck. We must keep her here. She's too mean spirited to roam about unrestrained. We are in agreement on this point. But does not she, too, deserve basic freedoms? Must she be compelled to moral norms, not only in deed but in thought as well? It is here, in a prison for the willfully damned, with Nuck, that we must settle the question.

We are dedicated to the defense of freedom of speech.